Daniel

This edition published by Parragon in 2012
Parragon
Queen Street House
4 Queen Street
Bath BA1 1HE, UK
www.parragon.com

ISBN 978-1-4454-7796-1

Printed in China

The Gingerbread Man

Retold by Louise Martin

Illustrated by Gail Yerrill

Parragon

Bath • New York • Singapore • Hong Kong • Cologne • Delhi
Melbourne • Amsterdam • Johannesburg • Auckland • Shenzhen

Once upon a time, a little old man and a little old woman lived in a cottage near the river.

One morning, the little old woman decided to bake a gingerbread man as a special treat.

You will need:
3½ cups (350g) all purpose flour
¾ cup (175g) light brown sugar
7 tablespoons (100g) butter
1 egg
4 tablespoons corn syrup
1 teaspoon baking powder
1½ teaspoons ground ginger
rolling pin
gingerbread man-shaped cookie cutter

The little old woman mixed together all the ingredients to make the gingerbread dough.

Then she rolled the dough out flat and used the cutter to make it into the shape of a little man.

Finally, she made some icing for his eyes and mouth, and she gave him three currant buttons and a cherry for a nose.
The gingerbread man was ready to be baked.

Half an hour later, the gingerbread man was baked and the little old woman opened the oven.

Suddenly, the gingerbread man jumped up and ran through the open kitchen door.

"Stop!" cried the old woman, running after him. "I want to eat you."

But the gingerbread man wouldn't stop. He didn't want to be eaten.

"Run, run as fast as you can.
You can't catch me,
I'm the gingerbread man!" he chanted.

The gingerbread man ran past the little old man.

"Stop!" cried the little old man. "I want to eat you."

But the gingerbread man ran even faster.

"I've run away from a little old woman and I can run away from you," he said.

"Run, run as fast
as you can.
You can't catch me,
I'm the gingerbread man!"
he chanted.

The little old man and the little old woman chased the gingerbread man into the yard, but he was too fast.

As he ran, he passed a pig.

"Stop!" snorted the pig. "I want to eat you."

But the gingerbread man ran even faster.

"I've run away from a little old woman and a little old man, and I can run away from you," he said.

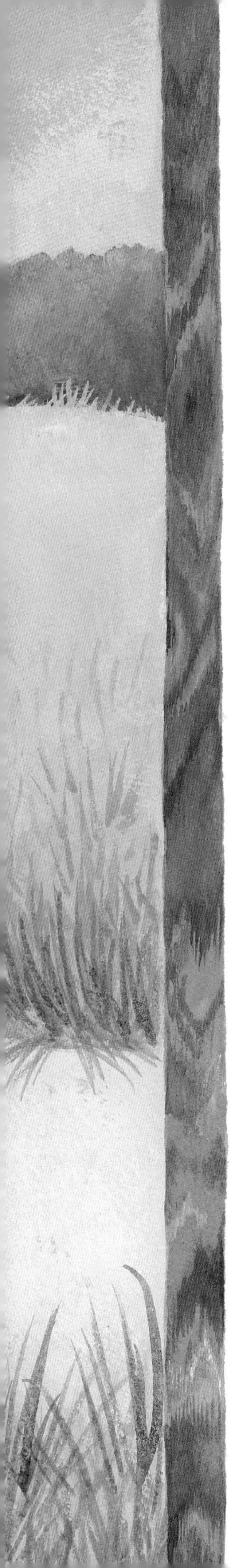

"Run, run as fast as you can.
You can't catch me,
I'm the gingerbread man!" he chanted.

The pig chased the gingerbread man, followed by the little old man and the little old woman.

The gingerbread man ran past a cow by the barn.

"Stop!" mooed the cow. "I want to eat you."

"I've run away from a little old woman, a little old man, and a pig, and I can run away from you," the gingerbread man cried.

"Run, run as fast as you can.
You can't catch me,
I'm the gingerbread man!" he chanted.

The cow, the pig, and the little old man and the little old woman all chased the gingerbread man. But the gingerbread man was too fast.

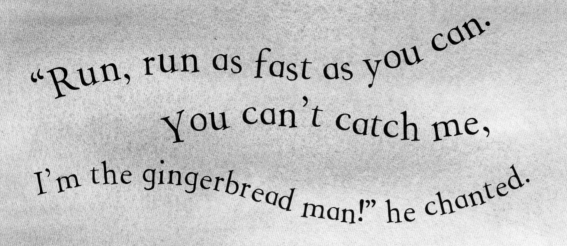

The gingerbread man raced past a horse in the field.

"Stop!" neighed the horse. "I want to eat you."

"I've run away from a little old woman, a little old man, a pig, and a cow, and I can run away from you," he said.

"Run, run as fast as you can.
You can't catch me,
I'm the gingerbread man!" he chanted.

The horse chased the gingerbread man, followed by ...

the cow,

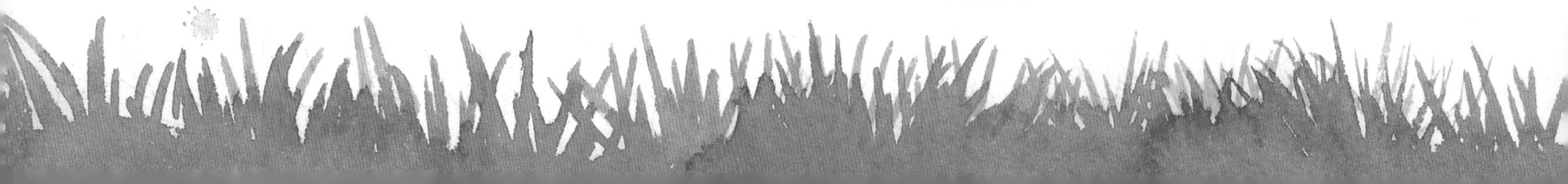

the pig,

the little old man,

and the little
old woman.

But the gingerbread
man was too fast.

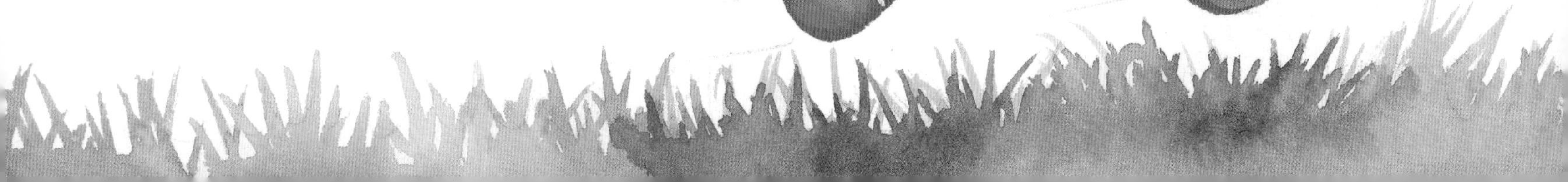

Then the gingerbread man reached
a river and stopped.

The sparkly water swirled in front of him.

"Oh, no! I can't swim," he cried.
"How will I get across?"

A sly and hungry fox saw the gingerbread man and licked his lips.

"Jump onto my tail and I will take you across the river," he said.

So the gingerbread man jumped onto the fox's tail.

After swimming halfway, the fox said, “You’re too heavy for my tail, jump onto my back.”

So the gingerbread man ran along the fox’s bushy tail and jumped onto his back.

After a while, the fox cried, "You're too heavy for my back. Jump onto my nose."

So the gingerbread man jumped onto the fox's nose.

But as soon as they reached the riverbank, the fox flipped the gingerbread man up into the air,

snapped his mouth shut and gobbled him up.

And that was the end of the gingerbread man!

The End